Here's what kids have to say to
Mary Pope Osborne, author of
the Magic Tree House series:

*Your books are so, so, so magical that I refuse
to get any other books from the library.*
—Ben H.

*I love the Magic Tree House books. My Daddy
and I have read all of them.*—Kevin F.

Me and my Mom really love your books.
—Julie P.

*Every time I finish your books I want to read
them over and over again because it is so
much fun.*—Soo Jin K.

*I'm going to write just like you when I grow
up.*—Raul A.

*Out of all the books in the world, yours are the
best. I hope your books will never end.*
—Karina D.

*You could really read my mind—wherever
Jack and Annie go, I want to go.*
—Matthew D.

Parents and teachers love Magic Tree House books, too!

I wish to thank you for creating this series, as you have given every teacher who passionately loves to read a vehicle for enticing young children to discover the magic of books.—K. Salkaln

My students <u>love</u> your Magic Tree House books. In fact, there is a reading craze in our classroom, thanks to your wonderful books! —S. Tcherepnin

I would like to say that your books are wonderful. I have never found any other educational books that were so interesting to my students.—C. Brewer

Kevin got two of your books with a gift certificate. He read the whole way home and did not come up for air until he had completed both books.—K. Trostle

I have been trying for years to find a book that students would enjoy and be crazy about. Most books do not capture the attention of students like your books do. Even my boys say, "Please do not stop reading." It is a pleasure to find something the students will read that is worthwhile and wholesome. I applaud you.
—L. Kirl

You have opened the door to adventures for some, and others want to follow in your footsteps as authors. Thank you for creating and sharing that magical world of the imagination.—M. Hjort

My son has always struggled when reading. Since discovering your books, he has a new desire to read.—M. Casameny

Dear Readers,

A while ago, I began researching the Arctic because so many of you wanted Jack and Annie to go there. When I came across a certain astonishing fact, I got very excited about writing the story. The fact was this: <u>Even though polar bears can weigh as much as 1,000 pounds, they can walk on ice that is too thin to hold a person!</u> How do they do this? They lie flat on the ice and <u>perfectly</u> balance their weight so that the ice won't crack. Then they move forward by pulling with their claws, all the while maintaining their perfect balance.

As you'll see, this particular fact, combined with my imagination, helped me plot the story.

So if you were to ask me where I get the inspiration for my Magic Tree House books, I'd have to say: readers, research, and my imagination. <u>And</u> I get further inspiration from my editor, Mallory Loehr, who has worked on all the books with me. She and I have fun meetings in which we go over and over the ideas for each book.

I hope you enjoy reading <u>Polar Bears Past Bedtime</u> as much as I enjoyed researching and writing it. And I hope it will inspire you to try researching and writing your <u>own</u> book.

All best,

E   #12

Polar Bears
Past Bedtime

by Mary Pope Osborne
illustrated by Sal Murdocca

A STEPPING STONE BOOK

Random House 🏠 New York

For Mallory Loehr
with gratitude for taking the journey
twelve times.

www.randomhouse.com/kids
www.magictreehouse.com

Library of Congress Cataloging-in-Publication Data
Osborne, Mary Pope. Polar bears past bedtime / by Mary Pope Osborne ;
illustrated by Sal Murdocca.
    p. cm. — (Magic tree house ; #12) "A Stepping Stone book."
Summary: Their magic tree house takes Jack and Annie to the Arctic, where
a polar bear leads them onto very thin ice.
ISBN 978-0-679-88341-8 (pbk.) — ISBN 978-0-679-98341-5 (lib. bdg.)
[1. Polar bear—Fiction. 2. Arctic regions—Fiction. 3. Magic—Fiction.
4. Tree houses—Fiction.]
I. Murdocca, Sal, ill. II. Title. III. Series: Osborne, Mary Pope. Magic tree house
series ; #12. PZ7.O81167Po 1998 [E]—dc21 97-15624

Printed in the United States of America 54 53 52

Random House, Inc. New York, Toronto, London, Sydney, Auckland

Contents

Polar Bears
Past Bedtime

1

Are You Serious?

Whoo. The strange sound came from outside the open window.

Jack opened his eyes in the dark.

The sound came again. *Whoo.*

Jack sat up and turned on his light. He put on his glasses. Then he grabbed the flashlight from his table and shone it out the window.

A white snowy owl was sitting on a tree branch.

"*Whoo,*" the owl said again. Its large

1

yellow eyes looked right into Jack's.

What does he want? Jack wondered. *Is he a sign, like the rabbit and the gazelle?*

A long-legged rabbit and a gazelle had led Jack and Annie to the magic tree house for their last two adventures.

"*Whoo.*"

"Wait a second," Jack said to the owl. "I'll get Annie."

Jack's sister, Annie, always seemed to know what birds and animals were saying.

Jack jumped out of bed and hurried to Annie's room. She was sound asleep.

Jack shook her and she stirred.

"What?" she said.

"Come to my room," whispered Jack. "I think Morgan's sent another sign."

In a split second, Annie was out of bed.

She hurried with Jack to his room.

Jack led her to the window. The snowy owl was still there.

"*Whoo*," said the owl. Then he raised his white wings and took off into the night.

"He wants us to go to the woods," said Annie.

"That's what I thought," said Jack. "Meet you downstairs after we get dressed."

"No, no. He says *go now*. Right now," said Annie. "We'll have to wear our pajamas."

"I *have* to put on my sneakers," said Jack.

"Okay, I'll put on mine, too. Meet you downstairs," said Annie.

Jack pulled on his sneakers. He threw his notebook into his backpack. Then he grabbed his flashlight and tiptoed downstairs.

Annie was waiting at the front door. They

silently slipped outside together.

The night air was warm. Moths danced around the porch light.

"I feel weird," said Jack. "I'm going back to put on some real clothes."

"You can't," said Annie. "The owl said *right now*."

She jumped off the porch and headed across their dark yard.

Jack groaned. *How did Annie know exactly what the owl said?* he wondered.

Still, he didn't want to be left behind. So he took off after her.

The moon lit their way as they ran down their street. When they entered the Frog Creek woods, Jack turned on his flashlight.

The beam of light showed shadows and swaying branches.

Jack and Annie stepped between the trees. They stayed close together.

"*Whoo.*"

Jack jumped in fear.

"It's just the white owl," said Annie. "He's somewhere nearby."

"The woods are creepy," said Jack.

"Yeah," said Annie. "In the dark, it doesn't even feel like our woods."

Suddenly the owl flapped near them.

"Yikes!" said Annie.

Jack shone his flashlight on the white bird as it rose into the sky. The owl landed on a tree branch—*right next to the magic tree house.*

And there was Morgan le Fay, the enchantress librarian. Her long white hair gleamed in the beam of Jack's flashlight.

"Hello," Morgan called softly in a soothing voice. "Climb up."

Jack used his flashlight to find the rope ladder. Then he and Annie climbed up into the tree house.

Morgan was holding three scrolls. Each one held the answer to an ancient riddle that Jack and Annie had already solved.

"You have journeyed to the ocean, the Wild West, and Africa to find the answers to these three riddles," said Morgan. "Ready for another journey?"

"Yes!" said Jack and Annie together.

Morgan pulled a fourth scroll from the folds of her robe. She handed it to Annie.

"After we solve this riddle, will we become Master Librarians?" asked Annie.

"And help you gather books through time

and space?" said Jack.

"Almost…" said Morgan.

Before Jack could ask what she meant, Morgan pulled out a book and gave it to him. "For your research," she said.

Jack and Annie looked at the book's title: ADVENTURE IN THE ARCTIC.

"Oh, wow, the Arctic!" said Annie.

"The *Arctic?*" said Jack. He turned to Morgan. "Are you serious?"

"Indeed I am," she said. "And you must hurry."

"I wish we could go there," said Annie, pointing at the cover.

"Wait—wait a minute—we'll freeze to death!" said Jack.

"Fear not," said Morgan. "I am sending someone to meet you."

The wind started to blow.

"Meet us? Who?" said Jack.

"*Whoo?*" said the snowy owl.

Before Morgan could answer, the tree house started to spin.

It spun faster and faster.

Then everything was still.

Absolutely still.

2

The Howling

The air was crisp and cold.

Jack and Annie shivered. They looked out the window at a dark gray sky.

The tree house was on the ground. There were no trees and no houses—only an endless field of ice and snow. Morgan and the owl were gone.

"R-r-read the riddle," said Annie, her teeth chattering.

Jack unrolled the scroll. He read:

> I cover what's real
> and hide what's true.
> But sometimes I bring out
> the courage in you.
> What am I?

"I'd better write it down," said Jack, shivering.

He pulled out his notebook and copied the riddle. Then he opened the book. He found a picture of a barren white field. He read aloud:

> The Arctic tundra is a treeless plain.
> During the dark winter, it is covered
> with snow and ice. In early spring,
> snow falls, but the sky begins to get
> lighter. During the summer season, the
> snow and ice melt and the sun shines
> 24 hours a day.

"It must be early spring now," said Jack. "There's snow, but the sky is a little light."

He turned the page. There was a picture of a man wearing a hooded coat with fur trim.

"Look at this guy," said Jack. He showed Annie the picture.

"We need his coat," said Annie.

"Yeah," said Jack. "Listen to this…"

He read aloud:

> This seal hunter wears sealskin clothing to protect him from icy winds. Before modern times, native people of the Arctic lived by hunting seals, caribou, polar bears, and whales.

Jack took out his notebook. He wrote:

THE ARCTIC

Seal hunters wear sealskin

He was too cold to write any more.

He clutched his pack against his chest and blew on his fingers. He wished he were back home in bed.

"Morgan said someone was coming to meet us," said Annie.

"If they don't come soon, we'll freeze to death," said Jack. "It's getting darker and colder."

"Shh. Listen," said Annie.

A howling sound came from the distance...then more howling sounds...and more.

"What's that?" said Jack.

They looked out the window. Snow was falling now. It was hard to see.

The howling grew louder. It was mixed with yipping and yelping noises. Jack and

Annie saw dark shapes coming through the snow. They seemed to be running toward the tree house.

"Wolves?" said Annie.

"Great. That's all we need," said Jack. "We're freezing, and now a pack of wolves is coming for us."

Jack pulled Annie into the corner of the tree house. They huddled close together.

The howling got louder and louder. It sounded as if the wolves were circling the tree house. They whined and yelped.

Jack couldn't stand it any longer. He grabbed the Arctic book.

"Maybe this can help us," he said.

He searched for a picture of wolves.

"Oh—hi!" Annie said.

Jack looked up. He caught his breath.

A man was looking through the tree house window. His face was surrounded by fur.

It was the seal hunter from the Arctic book.

3

Mush!

"Did you come with the wolves?" asked Annie.

The seal hunter looked puzzled.

"Did Morgan send you to us?" said Jack.

"I had a dream," the man said. "You were in it. You needed help."

Annie smiled.

"Morgan sends dreams sometimes," she said. "We came in Morgan's tree house. It flies through time."

Oh, brother, thought Jack. *Who will believe that?*

The seal hunter smiled as if he was not surprised at all.

"We do need help," said Jack. "W-w-we're fr-fr-freezing."

The seal hunter nodded. Then he left the

window. He returned a moment later with two small parkas like his own. They were made of heavy dark skins with fur-trimmed hoods.

He passed one to Jack and one to Annie.

"Thanks!" said Jack and Annie.

They put the parkas on.

"Hooray!" said Annie. "It's warm!"

"Yeah," said Jack. "They're made of seal-skin."

"Poor seals," said Annie.

"Don't think about it," said Jack. He pulled his hood up. His head and upper body were very snug now. Only his legs, hands, and feet were still freezing.

"Oh, thanks!" said Annie.

Jack looked up. The seal hunter was giving Annie a pair of fur pants. Then he handed a pair to Jack.

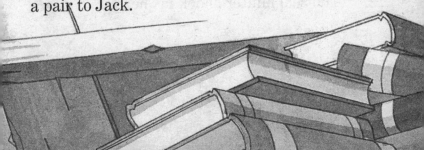

"Thanks," said Jack. He quickly pulled the pants on over his pajamas.

Next the seal hunter gave each of them a pair of fur boots and mittens.

Jack took off his sneakers and pulled on the boots. He wiggled his frozen fingers into the warm mittens.

"I have a quick question," Jack said to the seal hunter. "Do you know the answer to this riddle?"

He opened his notebook and read:

> I cover what's real
> and hide what's true.
> But sometimes I bring out
> the courage in you.
> What am I?

The seal hunter shook his head.

"Come," he said to Jack and Annie. Then he disappeared from the window.

"What about those wolves out there?" Jack called.

But the seal hunter didn't answer.

Jack grabbed the Arctic book and looked for a picture of the seal hunter.

When Jack found the picture, he smiled. The seal hunter was standing beside a dog-sled.

Jack read:

> In cold weather, the seal hunter travels by dogsled. Siberian Huskies often howl like wolves. A lead dog controls the others. The sled's runners are sometimes made of frozen fish rolled up in sealskin.

"Hey, Annie, they're not wolves," said

Jack. "They're—" He looked up.

Annie was gone.

Jack threw the book and notebook into his pack. But he was so fat in his furry clothes that the backpack wouldn't fit. Jack loosened the shoulder straps and tried to put the backpack on again. It fit.

Jack looked at the small window. That would be a tight fit, too. He went out head-first and barely squeezed through.

Jack fell onto the snowy ground. The snow was still drifting down. The air was misty white.

Jack heard barking and howling. He moved carefully toward the noise.

At first, he couldn't see the dogsled. But when he got closer, he counted nine Siberian Huskies. They had thick fur, big heads, and pointy ears.

The lead dog barked at him.

Jack stopped.

"He's telling you to climb on!" said Annie.

She was standing on the back of the sled. The seal hunter stood next to her in the snow.

Jack jumped onto the sled next to Annie.

The seal hunter cracked a long whip. "Mush!" he shouted.

The huskies dashed off in a whirl of snow.

Above them flew the snowy owl.

4

Snow House

The dogsled skimmed silently over the frozen tundra. The seal hunter ran alongside it. Sometimes he cracked his whip against the ice.

The snowdrifts looked like giant white sculptures as the sun slipped behind the frozen hills. Then a full orange moon rose in the sky.

The moonlight lit a small, rounded igloo in front of them. The dogs slowed, then stopped.

Jack stepped off the sled. Annie went to help unhitch the dogs. Jack took his book out and read about igloos:

> The word "igloo" means "house" in the language of native Arctic people. The house is built with blocks of snow. Dry snow is good wall material because it keeps in the heat. The temperature inside an igloo can be 65 degrees warmer than the temperature outside.

Jack took out his notebook. He pulled off his mitten just long enough to write:

igloo means house

"Come on, Jack!" said Annie.

She and the seal hunter were waiting for him in front of the igloo. The dogs were leashed together outside.

Jack hurried to join them. The hunter pushed aside animal skins covering the entrance. They stepped inside.

A fat candle burned brightly. Shadows danced on walls of ice and snow.

Jack and Annie sat on a fur-covered platform. They watched as the seal hunter moved about.

First he lit a small stove. Then he slipped outside. He came back with a snowball and chunks of frozen meat.

He put the snowball in a pot over the stove. Then he added the meat.

"What's he making?" asked Annie.

Jack pulled out his book and found a picture of the hunter cooking. He and Annie read the words silently:

There was a time when nearly all of the Arctic people's food and clothing and tools came from Arctic animals, especially the seal. Nearly every part of the seal could be eaten. Lamps were fueled with seal fat. Clothing was made from sealskin. And knives and needles were carved from seal bones.

"He must be boiling seal meat," said Jack.

"The poor seals," said Annie.

The seal hunter looked up.

"They are not poor," he said. "They help us because they know we would die without them."

"Oh," said Annie.

"In return, we always thank the animal spirits," said the seal hunter.

"How do you do that?" said Jack.

"We have many special ceremonies," said the seal hunter.

He reached under the fur-covered platform and took out two wooden masks.

"Soon there will be a ceremony to honor the spirit of the polar bear," he said. "I carved these masks for the ceremony."

"Polar bears?" said Annie.

"Yes," said the hunter. "Just as the seal has given us many gifts, so has the polar bear."

"Like what?" said Jack.

"Long ago the polar bear taught us how to live in the ice and snow," said the seal hunter.

"*Taught* you?" said Jack. "I mean, can you give us some facts?"

The seal hunter smiled.

"Yes," he said. "A polar bear catches a seal when the seal comes up to breathe through a hole in the ice. The oldest seal hunters watched the polar bear and learned. This is how my father taught me to hunt seal, as his father taught him."

"That's a good fact," said Jack.

"The very first of my people learned to make igloos from polar bears," said the hunter. "Polar bears build snow houses by digging caves in the drifts."

"Another good fact," said Jack.

"Sometimes the polar bear can even teach people to fly," said the seal hunter.

"That's an amazing fact," said Annie.

Jack smiled. "The rest sounded like true facts," he said. "But I know that's pretend."

The hunter just laughed, then turned back to his cooking.

That's why he wasn't surprised to hear about the tree house, Jack thought. *If he believes polar bears can fly, he probably would believe anything.*

The seal hunter lifted the chunks of boiled seal out of his pot. He dropped them into a wooden bucket and gave it to Annie.

"Let's feed the dogs," he said.

"Oh, boy!" said Annie. She followed the hunter outside, swinging the bucket.

Jack quickly threw his notebook and the Arctic book into his pack. He started to follow them. Then his gaze fell on the two bear masks.

He picked them up to get a better look.

Each was carved in the shape of a polar bear's face with a blunt nose and roundish ears. There were two holes for eyes and a strap to hold it on your head.

Suddenly howls split the air. The dogs were barking and growling. Annie squealed.

Are the dogs attacking her? Jack wondered.

"Annie!"

Still holding the bear masks, Jack charged out of the igloo.

5

You're It!

The dogs were barking wildly at two small creatures playing in the moonlight.

"Polar bear babies!" cried Annie.

One roly-poly cub leaped onto the other. Then they both rolled through the snow.

"Hi, little bears!" Annie called.

The cubs jumped up and shook themselves like wet puppies. Then they scampered toward Annie, who rushed to greet them.

"Hi, hi, hi!" she called.

"Wait—" shouted Jack. "Where's their mother?"

He looked around for the mother bear, but she was nowhere in sight. *Maybe they're orphans,* he thought.

Jack looked back at Annie. She was wrestling with the little bears in the snow. She was laughing so hard that she couldn't stand.

Jack started laughing, too. He carefully put the bear masks into his pack. Then he ran to join Annie.

She was running with the cubs across the snowy tundra. One of them raced to her, tagged her, then raced away. Annie ran after the bear and tagged him back.

"You're it!" she said.

Jack and the other cub joined in. Soon

Jack and Annie and the two cubs were all chasing each other over the moonlit snow.

They ran until the two cubs fell down ahead of them. The cubs lay perfectly still.

Panting, Jack and Annie stared at them.

"Are they hurt?" Annie wondered out loud.

Jack and Annie ran to the cubs.

Then, just as they leaned down to see if they were all right, the cubs jumped up. They pushed Jack and Annie over and scampered away.

"They were pretending!" said Jack. He laughed.

Jack and Annie charged after the cubs. They ran over the white tundra until they came to the frozen sea.

Jack looked around.

"We're pretty far from the igloo. I don't

hear the huskies anymore," he said. "Maybe we should go back."

"In a minute," said Annie. "Look!"

The bear cubs had scooted up a snowbank. They were on their backs, sliding down the bank onto the ice-covered sea.

Jack and Annie laughed.

"It's like sledding!" said Annie. "Let's try it!"

"Okay," said Jack, "but then we have to go back."

Jack followed Annie up the snowbank. He clutched his pack in his arms.

Annie lay on her back. She whooped as she slid down the ice.

Jack followed her.

"Watch out below!" he shouted.

The little bears were sitting at the bottom

of the snowbank. One gently whapped Jack in the face with her furry paw. Then she lay down.

"I'm tired, too," said Annie.

"Yeah," said Jack. "Let's rest for just a minute."

Jack and Annie looked up at the orange moon as they lay beside the cubs. All they could hear was the wind and the soft breathing of the cubs.

"That was *fun*," said Annie.

"It was," said Jack. "But we'd better head back to the igloo. The seal hunter's probably looking for us. Plus we have to solve the riddle."

Jack rolled onto his side and tried to stand. *Crack.*

"Uh-oh," he said. He went back down onto

his knees. "I think we're on thin ice."

"What do you mean?" said Annie. She started to stand.

Another *crack* rang out.

"Uh-oh," she said.

She carefully lay back down.

The polar bear cubs moved closer to Jack and Annie. They made little crying sounds.

Jack wanted to cry, too. But he took a deep breath.

"Let's see what our book says," he said.

He reached into his pack for the Arctic book. He took the masks out first and handed them to Annie.

"I took these from the igloo by mistake," he said.

As he started to reach for his Arctic book, he heard the loudest crack of all.

CRACK!

"We're not even moving and the ice is cracking," said Annie.

Just then, there was a new sound—a low, snorting sound. It came from the top of the snowbank, about fifty feet away.

Jack looked up.

Staring down at them was a giant polar bear.

"The polar bear mother," whispered Annie.

6

Flying Bears

The cubs whimpered louder.

"They want to go to her, but they're afraid of the ice," whispered Jack.

Annie petted the cubs.

"Don't be afraid," she told them. "You'll get back to your mother."

The big polar bear growled. She paced back and forth, sniffing the air.

Annie kept patting the two cubs and whispering to them.

Jack looked in the book for anything that might help. Finally he found something:

> **Even though a female polar bear can weigh as much as 750 pounds, she can walk on ice too thin to hold a person by balancing her weight and sliding her paws over the ice.**

"Oh, man, that's incredible," whispered Jack.

He watched the mother polar bear walk down the snowbank.

On large silent feet, she crept about at the edge of the frozen sea.

She tried to step onto the ice. But each time she did, it cracked, and she had to retreat. At last, she found a firm spot.

Then the polar bear stretched out her four legs and lay on the ice. Slowly she moved forward, pushing herself with her claws.

"Is she coming for her babies?" said Jack. "Or is she coming to get *us?*"

"I don't know," said Annie. "Hey, let's put on the masks."

"What for?" said Jack.

"Maybe they'll protect us," said Annie. "Maybe she'll think we're polar bears, too."

"Oh, brother," said Jack.

But Annie gave him a bear mask. He took off his glasses and slipped it on.

Jack peered through the mask holes. It was hard to see the huge white bear sliding over the frozen sea. He squinted. That helped.

The polar bear looked at her cubs and let out a deep moan.

The two little bears carefully went to their mother. She licked the cubs and touched her nose against each of theirs. Then they crawled onto her back.

"They're safe now," said Jack. "Even if the mother breaks through the ice, she can swim with them to the shore."

"Yeah, I just wish she wouldn't leave *us* behind," said Annie.

The mother bear slowly turned her body around. Then she pushed off with her hind legs. With her cubs on her back, she began sliding away.

"Let's try moving like her," Annie said.

"But we could break through and freeze to death," said Jack.

"If we just stay here, we'll freeze, too," said Annie. "Remember, the seal hunter said his people had learned from the polar bears."

Jack took a deep breath.

"Okay," he said. "Let's try it."

He lay on his stomach. He spread out his arms and legs.

Then he copied the bear. He pressed his

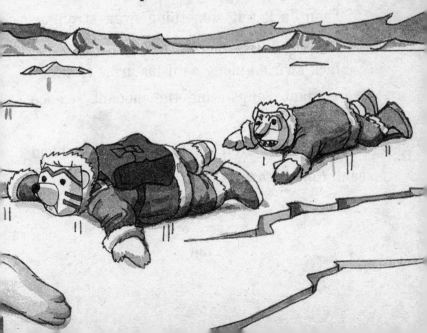

mittens against the ice and pushed off, sliding his feet.

Amazingly, there was no cracking sound.

"*Grrr*," he growled. And he pushed off again.

Jack heard Annie sliding behind him. He kept going. He pushed and slid. He pushed again and slid again.

He made the movements over and over, until something happened: He didn't feel like a boy anymore. He felt like a polar bear.

Then Jack felt something even stranger. He felt like a *flying* polar bear.

Jack swirled along as if his arms and legs were giant wings—and the moonlit sea ice were a glassy sky.

He remembered what the seal hunter had said: *Polar bears can fly.*

7

Spirit Lights

"Jack, you can get up now," said Annie.

Jack opened his eyes. Annie was standing over him. She still had her mask on.

"We're on safe ground," she said.

Jack felt as if he'd been dreaming. He looked around. They had reached the tundra at the edge of the frozen sea.

The cubs were romping in the distance. But their mother was sitting nearby, gazing at Jack and Annie.

"She waited to make sure we were safe," said Annie.

Jack stared at the polar bear in awe. The words of the seal hunter came back to him: *Always thank the animal spirits.*

"We should thank the polar bear spirit now," he said.

"Of course," said Annie.

Jack scrambled to his feet. Still wearing his bear mask, he stood before the polar bear and pressed his hands together.

"We thank you," he said, bowing.

"Yes, we thank you forever," said Annie, also bowing.

"We thank you beyond the moon and the stars," said Jack.

"And beyond the deepest sea," Annie added.

Then she threw out her arms and twirled around. Jack did the same. They both danced around in the snow, honoring the bear. Finally they stopped and bowed one last time.

When they looked up, the polar bear rose up on her hind legs. She was twice as tall as Jack. She lowered her huge head, as if she were bowing back to them.

At that moment, the sky exploded. The night became a giant swirl of red, green, and purple lights. It looked like a genie coming out of a magic lamp.

The sight took Jack's breath away. He stared in wonder as the dazzling lights lit the tundra.

"Is it the polar bear spirit?" Annie asked in a hushed voice.

As far as Jack could see, the sky and snow

shimmered. Even the bear's fur shimmered in the strange light.

"No, it's not a spirit," said Jack. "There's got to be a scientific reason. I'll find out."

Shaking, he reached into his backpack and pulled out the Arctic book. He took off his bear mask and put on his glasses.

By the greenish glow, Jack found a picture of the sky lights. The picture didn't come close to the real thing. He read aloud:

> One of the most amazing sights in the Arctic is the northern lights. The swirl of light is caused by electrically charged particles from the sun striking atoms and molecules in the earth's atmosphere.

"See, there *is* a scientific reason!" said Jack. "It's not the spirits."

Then suddenly all the dancing lights were gone, as if someone had blown out a candle.

The magic had ended.

8

Riddle Solved

Now only the moon shone on the snow.

Jack looked around for the polar bear.

She was gone.

"Where'd she go?" asked Annie.

"I don't know," said Jack. He looked over the tundra. There was no sign of the giant bear or her cubs.

"Maybe she's not interested in scientific reasons," Jack said.

Annie sighed. She took off her bear mask

and handed it to Jack. He put both their masks in his pack.

"Now what?" asked Annie.

They looked around. The vast fields of snow ended in darkness. Jack had no idea where they were.

He shrugged. "I guess we just have to walk and hope for the best."

"Wait—listen," said Annie.

From the distance came howling sounds. They grew louder and louder.

"Yay! We don't have to wait long!" said Annie. "The huskies are coming!"

Howling filled the night as the dogsled came into view.

The seal hunter was running beside it.

"We're here! Over here!" called Jack. He ran toward the sled. Annie followed.

"I was afraid you were lost," said the seal hunter.

"We were!" said Annie. "And we got stuck on thin ice, too! But a polar bear helped us."

"Yeah," said Jack. "And we wore your masks and they made us feel like bears—"

"Yeah, the masks made us brave," said Annie. She caught her breath.

"Oh, man, wait—" said Jack. Annie's words sounded familiar.

He took out his notebook and read Morgan's riddle aloud:

> I cover what's real
> and hide what's true.
> But sometimes I bring out
> the courage in you.
> What am I?

"A mask!" Jack and Annie said together.

The seal hunter smiled.

"You knew!" said Annie.

"It was for you to discover," said the seal hunter. "Not me."

Jack pulled the bear masks out of his backpack.

"Here," he said. "Thanks a lot."

The hunter took the masks and put them inside his parka.

"We can go home now," said Jack.

"Do you mind taking us back to the tree house?" said Annie.

The seal hunter shook his head.

"Climb on," he said.

Jack and Annie climbed onto the dogsled.

"Mush!" said the seal hunter.

"Mush!" said Annie.

"Mush!" said Jack.

Snow began to fall as they took off across the dark ice.

9

Oh, No, One More!

By the time the dogsled arrived at the tree house, the snowstorm had become a blizzard.

"Can you wait just a minute?" Jack asked the seal hunter. "So we can check something?"

The hunter nodded. His dogs whined as Jack and Annie climbed through the tree house window.

Jack grabbed the scroll that held the riddle. He unrolled it. The riddle was gone. In its place was one shimmering word:

MASK

"We did it!" said Annie. "The tree house will take us home now."

"Great!" said Jack. "Let's say good-bye to the seal hunter and give him back his clothes."

They quickly pulled off their sealskin clothing and their boots.

"Thanks for letting us borrow these!" Jack called through the window.

The seal hunter walked to the tree house and took the clothes from Jack and Annie. They stood shivering in their pajamas and bare feet.

"Th-th-thanks for everything!" said Annie, her teeth chattering.

The seal hunter gave them a wave. Then

he walked through the swirling snow to his sled.

"Mush!" he shouted.

The dogs took off through the stormy night.

"Let's get out of here!" said Jack. He hugged himself. "Before we freeze to death!"

Annie grabbed the Pennsylvania book that always took them home. She pointed to a picture of the Frog Creek woods.

"I wish we could go there!" she said.

They waited for the tree house to start spinning.

Nothing happened.

Jack shivered.

"I wish we could go there!" Annie said again.

Again nothing happened.

"Wh-wh-what's going on?" said Jack.

He looked around the tree house. The four scrolls with the solved riddle answers were in the corner.

Then he saw it—a *fifth* scroll.

"Where did *th-th-that* come from?" he said.

Jack grabbed it and unrolled it. On it were the words:

> Look at the letters:
> the first, not the rest.
> Discover the place
> that you love the best.

"Oh, no!" said Annie. "Another riddle!"

"Okay, okay. Let's stay c-c-calm," Jack said, shivering. "*Look at the letters: the first, not the rest.* Okay, the first letters in this riddle are L-A-T-L-T—"

"That doesn't make any sense," Annie broke in.

Icy winds battered the tree house. Snow blew inside.

"We have to hurry!" said Annie.

Jack was freezing. He looked around wildly.

"Letters, letters, letters. *What* letters?" he said.

His gaze rested on the scrolls in the corner.

"M-m-maybe we should look at the letters of the *answers*," he said.

"Right," said Annie.

They began unrolling the scrolls.

The scroll from their adventure under the ocean said:

OYSTER

The scroll from their trip to the Wild West said:

ECHO

The scroll from their journey to Africa said:

HONEY

Their scroll from the Arctic said:

MASK

"Oyster, echo, honey, mask," said Jack. "Their first letters are O-E-H-M."

"That doesn't make any sense, either," said Annie.

"Yeah, but maybe we have to unscramble

those letters," said Jack. "O-E-H-M...They could spell *hemo*."

"Or *meho*," said Annie.

"Or *home!*" said Jack.

"HOME!" cried Annie. "That's the place we love the best!"

Jack unrolled the fifth scroll again. The riddle was gone. In its place was one shimmering word:

HOME

"Yay!" cried Annie. She grabbed the Pennsylvania book. "I wish we could go home! HOME! HOME! HOME!"

The tree house started to spin.

It spun faster and faster and faster.

Then everything was still.

Absolutely still.

10

Master Librarians

Warm air washed over Jack. It felt wonderful.

"You have succeeded in your quest," said a soft, soothing voice. "Are you glad to be home?"

Jack opened his eyes. Morgan le Fay stood in the moonlight.

"Yes," he said.

"We solved all our riddles," said Annie.

"Indeed," said Morgan. "You have proved

that you can find answers to very hard questions."

She reached into the folds of her robe and took out two thin pieces of wood.

"A magic library card for each of you," she said.

She gave one to Annie and one to Jack.

"Oh, man," said Jack, feeling the card.

The wooden card was as thin and smooth as an ordinary library card. On its surface shimmered the letters *M* and *L*.

"These are your Master Librarian cards," said Morgan. "You are the newest members of the ancient Society of Master Librarians."

"What do we do with them?" asked Jack.

"Take them on your future journeys," said Morgan. "Only a very wise person or another Master Librarian will be able to see the let

ters. These will be the people who can help you."

"Wow," said Annie. "Can we go on a mission right now?"

"Now you must go home and rest," said Morgan. "I will come back for you soon."

Jack and Annie put their secret cards in their pockets. Then Jack took out the Arctic book and put it with the other books.

"Good-bye," he said.

"See you soon," Annie said to Morgan.

Morgan gave them a little wave.

Jack and Annie climbed down the rope ladder.

As soon as they stepped onto the dark ground, they heard a roar. They looked up. They saw a blur of wind and light high in the oak tree.

Then all was silent.

Morgan and her magic tree house were gone.

Jack reached for his magic library card. When he felt its tingly warmth, he *knew* that amazing adventures lay ahead.

"Let's go," he said.

He turned on his flashlight.

"The woods don't feel scary like they did before," said Annie as they walked through the trees. "I'm not afraid anymore."

"Me neither," said Jack.

"Hey, the darkness is like a *mask*," said Annie.

"Yeah," said Jack. "It hides the day, but it brings out your courage."

They came out of the woods.

Jack saw their house in the distance. It looked warm and cozy.

The porch light glowed. The moon shone overhead.

"*Home*," he whispered.

"*Home*," said Annie.

She started running. Jack took off after her, running to the place that they both loved the best.

JACK'S FACTS ABOUT THE ARCTIC

In the summer the sun never sets.
In the winter the sun never rises.
Seal hunters wear sealskin.
Siberian Huskies pull dogsleds.
"Igloo" means "house."
People can learn from animals.
Polar bears can walk on ice too thin
to hold a person.
The northern lights are an amazing sight.

Want to learn more about polar bears and the Arctic?

Track down the facts behind the fiction with the Magic Tree House® Fact Tracker.

Available now!

Have you read the Magic Tree House book in which Jack and Annie run into lions on the plains of Africa?

MAGIC TREE HOUSE® #11

LIONS AT LUNCHTIME

Don't miss the next Magic Tree House book,
in which Jack and Annie find themselves
in hot water when they arrive in ancient
Rome during a volcanic eruption . . .

MAGIC TREE HOUSE® #13

VACATION UNDER
THE VOLCANO

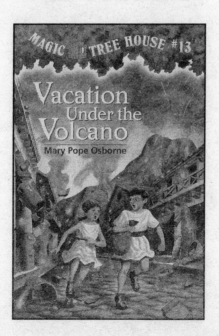

Around the World with Jack and Annie!

You have traveled to faraway places and have been
on countless Magic Tree House adventures.
Now is your chance to receive an official
Magic Tree House passport and collect official stamps
for each destination from around the world!

HOW

Get your exclusive Magic Tree House Passport!*

Send your name, street address, city, state, zip code, and date of birth to:
The Magic Tree House Passport, Random House Children's Books,
Marketing Department, 1745 Broadway, 10th Floor, New York, NY 10019

OR log on to www.magictreehouse.com
to download and print your passport now!

Collect Official Magic Tree House Stamps:

Log on to **www.magictreehouse.com** to submit your answers to the
trivia questions below. If you answer correctly, you will automatically
receive your official stamp for Book 12: *Polar Bears Past Bedtime*.

1. What animal leads Jack and Annie to the tree house
   at the beginning of the adventure?

2. What kind of house is built out of blocks of snow?

3. What do seal hunters wear to stay warm in the Arctic?

*One passport per person. No purchase necessary. While supplies last. Allow 6 to 8 weeks for delivery.